EIGHTH GRADE

GRADE

IS MAKING ME

SICK

Also by Jennifer L. Holm

The Babymouse series
(with Matthew Holm)

Boston Jane: An Adventure

Boston Jane: Wilderness Days

Boston Jane: The Claim

Comics Squad: Recess (edited with
Matthew Holm and Jarrett J. Krosoczka)

The Creek

The Fourteenth Goldfish

Middle School Is Worse than Meatloaf

Our Only May Amelia

Penny from Heaven

The Squish series (with Matthew Holm)

The Trouble with May Amelia

Turtle in Paradise

EIGHTH GRADE
GRADE
IS MAKING ME
SICK

GINNY DAVIS'S YEAR IN STUFF

Ginny

A Yearling Book

BY Jennifer L. Holm

ILLUSTRATED BY Elicia Castaldi

Ginny's Big To-Do List

1. Try out for cheer
2. Convince Mom to let me bike to school
3. Fall in love
4. Work on art (sketch every day)
5. Save money
6. Look good in family Christmas photo
7. Join Vampire Vixens Den
8. Teach Grampa Joe how to email
9. Have a cool Halloween costume for once
10. Ignore horoscopes!

)(Pisces
Keep your eyes on the prize, Pisces!

1

Eden Valley Estates

By
Grenville Builders

Now offering LUXURY five-bedroom homes.
Luxury en suite master bath with Mediterranean tile show
Granite and stainless-steel appointments in kitchen.
3,700 square feet.
Media room with surround sound.
Buyer incentive!

*Final inspection
Sat @ 3pm
meet with realtor,
closing Tuesday
9:30 AM
@ bank*

SEPTEMBER

SUNDAY	MONDAY	TUESDAY	WEDNESDAY	THURSDAY	FRIDAY	SATURDAY
		1	2	3	4	5
6	7	8	9	10	11	12
13	14	15	16		18	19
20	21	22	23		25	26
27	28	29	30			

COUNTDOWN TO GRAMPA JOE

OCTOBER

SUNDAY	MONDAY	TUESDAY	WEDNESDAY	THURSDAY	FRIDAY	SATURDAY
				1	2	3
4	5	6	7	8	9	10
11	12	13	14	15	16	17
18	19	20	21	22	23	24
25	26	27	28	29	30	

NOVEMBER

	MONDAY	TUESDAY	WEDNESDAY	THURSDAY	FRIDAY	
	2	3	4	5	6	
	9	10	11	12	13	14
	16	17	18	19	20	21
	23	24	25	26	27	28
	30					

Thanksgiving

ATTENTION, HOUSEHOLD MEMBERS:

Stop slacking and get packing!

Ginny—Throw some stuff out!

Henry—That beanbag is not going to the new house. It smells like something curled up and died in it.

Bob—Please drop off Hoover at the kennel the night before. We can't have him peeing on the movers like he did to Timmy's little friend.

Sincerely,
The Management

P.S. The movers will be here at 7am sharp, people!!

GINNY

SAVE

GINNY

TOSS

3

WOODLAND BANK
"Your Hometown Bank"

ACCOUNT NO.
4357287

ACCOUNT TYPE
WORRY-FREE CHECKING

STATEMENT PERIOD
Aug. 1 - Aug. 31

Genevieve Davis
Melinda Davis-Wright (guardian)
2610 Lark Lane
Woodland Glen, PA 18762

Posting Date	Transaction Description	Deposits & Interest	Checks & Subtractions	Daily Balance
08-01	Beginning Balance			$25.00
08-05	Deposit	+ $40.00		$65.00
08-15	ATM		- $55.00	$10.00
08-??	Deposit	+ $28.00		$38.00
08-21	ATM		- $30.00	$8.00
08-31	Ending Balance			$8.00

ESSAYS

GinnyGirl

GinnyGirl

We r in!!! The cable guy finally
showed up! I have mi own bathroom!
I don't have 2 share with the
dixgusting boyz!

beckysooboo1

U r so luckey. Maybe I can use ur
bathroom, too? Pretty please? ☺

GinnyGirl

Tee-hee.

✎ WRITE   📷 PHOTO   😊 EMOTICON

SEND

JOKES

Dream Book

TASTE THE LEM

DIET
TOP
F

Crisp and R
Le
affeine free
NOW WITH MO

5

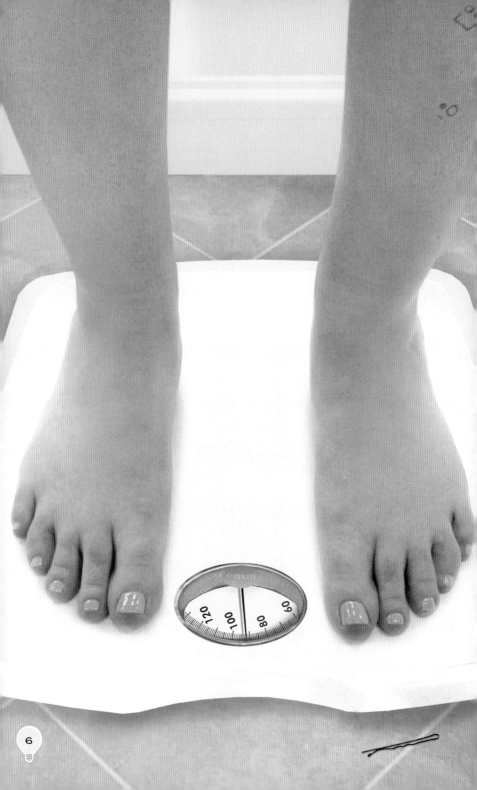

ggirl > Momcat:
Here's mi list 4 skool:
gim unifrm
new sneakurs
new bck pack
colored pencils for
art class

Momcat > ggirl:
And a dictionary,
CLEARLY. Do not go over
P.S. Do not go over
your texting minutes
this month.

GOOD

you're gonna need it!

Luck

HAVE A GREAT FIRST DAY OF SCHOOL.
XOXO GRAMPA JOE
(AKA THE OLD GUY IN FLORIDA)

SUNBURST

BLUSHING BRIDE

GOLDEN WHIMSY

LOLLIPOP LUNACY

CREAMSICLE

VIXEN PINK

CLOUD NINE

HIGH TIDE

PEACOCK DREAM

Ginny,
Pick a few colors
you would like for
your bedroom. And, no,
you may not have
black walls, even if
every Vampire Vixen in
the country has them.
Mom

HONEY

SMALL BATCH
BEAR
BUZZ

TUSCAN BLEND

CAFFÈ CASTALDI
TOSTATO A LEGNA

NATURA CIULIANA

Angelo Fifth Ave   ...ect-A-Vis...
18   +2.50

STUDENT HANDBOOK

WOODLAND CENTRAL MIDDLE SCHOOL

THE COUGARS' PRIDE

FROM THE DESK OF: Mrs. MacGillicuty

Dear Parents,

Please be reminded that students are not permitted to use or bring cell phones on school property. Any cell phones will be confiscated.

nk you.

MacGillicuty
pal

ND CENTRAL W C M S MIDDLE SCHOOL

Dear Eighth Graders and Parents:
Important Dates
Monday, August 24: First Day of School
Thursday, August 27: Back-to-School Night
Friday, September 11: Half-Day Teacher In-service
Thursday, September 17: School Book Fair

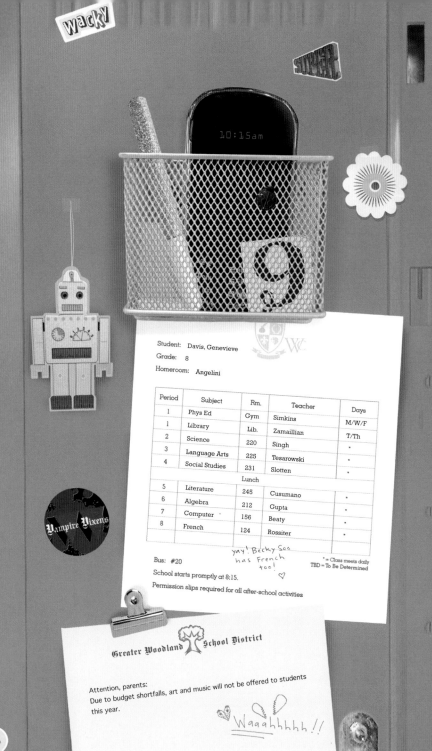

WACKY

SUPER

10:15am

Student: Davis, Genevieve

Grade: 8

Homeroom: Angelini

Period	Subject	Rm.	Teacher	Days
1	Phys Ed	Gym	Simkins	M/W/F
1	Library	Lib.	Zamaillian	T/Th
2	Science	220	Singh	"
3	Language Arts	225	Tesarowski	"
4	Social Studies	231	Slotten	"
	Lunch			
5	Literature	245	Cusumano	"
6	Algebra	212	Gupta	"
7	Computer	156	Beaty	"
8	French	124	Rossiter	"

yay! Becky Soo has French too! ♡

Bus: #20

* = Class meets daily
TBD = To Be Determined

School starts promptly at 8:15.

Permission slips required for all after-school activities

Greater Woodland School District

Attention, parents:
Due to budget shortfalls, art and music will not be offered to students this year.

Waaahhhhh!!

Vampire Vixens

10

<u>Awesome</u>!
is my new
language arts teacher's,
Ms. Tesarowski's,
favorite thing to say.
It's her first year
teaching and she thinks everything
about middle school is
<u>Awesome</u>!
She says kids our age
are creative
and inspirational and
<u>Awesome</u>!
She tells us that
getting paid to talk
about writing is
<u>Awesome</u>!

I wonder if <u>Awesome</u>!
will still be her favorite word
after she tries the
teriyaki beef blasters.
I'm thinking it actually
might be
<u>Gross</u>!

25
142

Pisces *February 19 to March 20*

An exciting project is on the horizon, Pisces!

FREAK OUT MAGAZINE PAGE 12

MOO JUICE
MADE WITH REAL MILK

want to be lab partners again? (I hear we're dissecting fetal pigs this year!) Awesome!!!! — Brian

13

Ginny!
We get 800 channels
now! Even the
Operation Channel!
I can't wait to see
the rhinoplasty
episode! And liposuction!
(I'll make the
popcorn with
EXTRA BUTTER!)
            -Henry

14

beckysooboo1

Did u get your mom's credit card
number so you can join VVV?
Once you log on, go to The Den!
It's so cool!

GinnyGirl

Bob gave me his number and I'm
setting up my character now.

beckysooboo1

I love ur step-bob! Want to come
over tomorrow after school??

GinnyGirl

I have 2 babysit Timmy. Mom's
defending the Sidewalk Guy.

beckysooboo1

I don't understand how you can sue
someone for slipping on ice???

GinnyGirl

Rite?? Mom sez she cant believe
she went to lawskool 4 this.

beckysooboo1

I know!! Let's go slip in front of
the movie theater! I bet they have
tons of money!!!!!!!!!!!!!!! Then
we could fly 2 California and go on
a studio tour for the new Vampire
Vixens movie!!!!

GinnyGirl

AWESOME!!!!!!!!!!!!!!!!!!!!!!!!!
LOL!!!!!!!!!!!!!!!

WRITE   PHOTO   EMOTICON

SEND

KEEP OUT!!! THIS MEANS U HENRY

Dream Book

FRESH POETRY INITIATIVE!

Dear 8th Graders,

As part of our Fresh Poetry Initiative, you will write a poem in class every Friday in Language Arts. This is to get you in the habit of freewriting poetry. At the end of the year, we will have a Poetry Slam.

Remember, poetry is . . .

F=Fun!
R=React!
E=Excite!
S=Share!
H=Hope!

Dumb Homework
① English: Read Animal Farm
② Algebra:
③ Social Studies:
Ch 1 Revolutionary
War read about a
bunch of dead people
who wore wigs.
③ French:
Un deux trois
I should have taken Spanish

Look, Mom!
Black is in!
Can I at least
have black + white
stripes??
Ginny

black is the new taupe

Ten Reasons to Fit Black
into Your Decorating Scheme

the Den

vixen: GinnyGirl

LOG OUT

MOOD: (unpacking!)

SHARE: pic / video

RAMBLING THOUGHTS: Bonjour, Mademoiselle Vixens! I need some decorating help!

FAILED IDEAS, ETC

vixen friends:

Becky Soo

Henry

vamp chat

I dink dis is da vorst vampire vixen movie evah. —SusietheBanshee

YOU ARE SO WRONG. —pixie

He should have kissed her. —Darling Clementine

NO WAY IT WAS PERFECT. —pixie

I am in love. —Claricelikesfavabeans

WHAT'S HIS NAME? —pixie

Garfield. —Claricelikesfavabeans

Like the cat??? —GinnyGirl

SAY IT!

playlist: Vampire Vixens Whole New World Movie Sound Track
Transylvania Troubadour
Stake Through My Heart (live)
The Future Is Ours (Bye-Bye Humans)
Too Busy Dying to Live
Everything Dead Is New

EDIT PROFILE >>

Dream Book

ROYAL ROOT BEER SODA POP

AL FROTHY MU

MORE FLAVOR!

COMMAND

17

Poetry Friday!

Assignment: Write a poem about school. Be sure to title your poem.
A title is the "icing on the cake."

"A Big Waste"

I think
getting up at six am
to eat cold cereal
so I can walk to the
bus stop by six forty-five
and wait for a bus
that shows up at seven-fifteen
to get to school
by seven forty-five
in order to wait in homeroom
until eight am
so I can listen to
dumb announcements
is pretty much
two whole hours
of my life
that are wasted
when I could be sleeping.
(Especially since I could bike
to school in like ten minutes
if my mom would let me!)

I hate getting up
early, too, Ginny!
Keep up the
awesome work!
Mr. T.

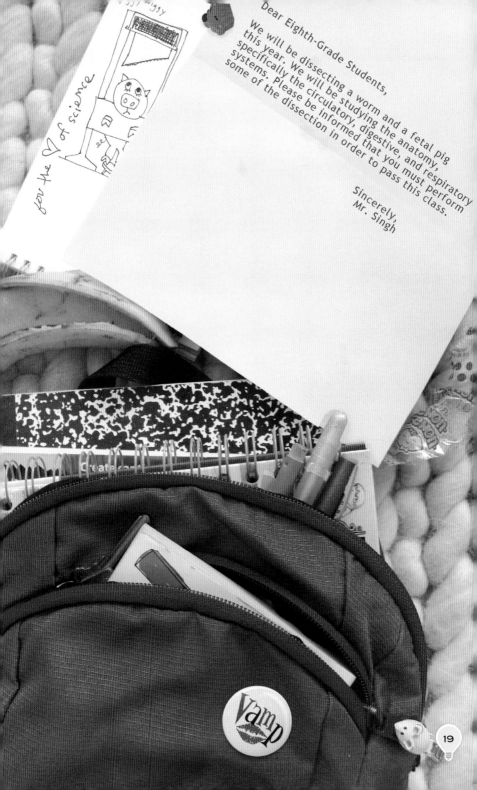

Dear Eighth-Grade Students,

We will be dissecting a worm and a fetal pig this year. We will be studying the anatomy, specifically the circulatory, digestive, and respiratory systems. Please be informed that you must perform some of the dissection in order to pass this class.

Sincerely,
Mr. Singh

for the ♥ of science

Extra Cheese
Sausage
Meatball
Mushroom
Pepperoni
Peppers
Onions
Anchovies
Customer
Spec
Other

Big Little Fruit   My name is Timmy

3 big apples

5 little apples

B's Shopping
Notebook $
Pineapple $2
Shampoo $5
Pizza $10
Bananas $2
n $1
ttuce $3
p $5

TOTAL

$3

LET'S LEARN "W"

Name Timmy

want   want want want

Dear Ginny,
I've got a late deposition and Bob's got
a dinner meeting with a new client. Please
make sure Timmy does his homework.
Get a pizza from Al's. Also, please
call me if Henry doesn't come home.
              Thanks, Mom
P.S. Do not do Timmy's homework for him!!
P.P.S. Don't forget to walk Hoover, and don't
let him off the leash again.
P.P.P.S. Yes, I will pay you.

white   white   white white

THE COMPLETE BITE:
An Unauthorized Guide to the Vampire Vixens

NIGHTBIRD PRESS

THE COMPLETE BITE:
An Unauthorized Guide to the Vampire Vixens

Markie PRECISION HIGHLIGHTER

GET'N GORG!
GLAM GLOSS

Eighth Grade Literature

Good to see so many of you again! I will be teaching 8th Grade Literature this year instead of 7th, so you get to enjoy me two years in a row. THE HOBBIT will be our class read, and you will be required to read two additional books from the list below each quarter and turn in a novel study. In addition, you will be required to do one author study. I look forward to an excellent year and many great discussions!

—Mr. Cusumano

Classics
Jane Eyre by Charlotte Brontë
The Count of Monte Cristo by Alexandre Dumas
The Diary of a Young Girl by Anne Frank
The Old Man and the Sea by Ernest Hemingway
A Wrinkle in Time by Madeleine L'Engle
Anne of Green Gables by L. M. Montgomery
Animal Farm by George Orwell
Dracula by Bram Stoker
Adventures of Huckleberry Finn by Mark Twain

Contemporary
Speak by Laurie Halse Anderson
Feed by M. T. Anderson
Ender's Game by Orson Scott Card
Hattie Big Sky by Kirby Larson
Monster by Walter Dean Myers
When My Name Was Keoko by Linda Sue Park
Monsoon Summer by Mitali Perkins
Rain Is Not My Indian Name by Cynthia Leitich Smith
Shiva's Fire by Suzanne Fisher Staples
Stuck in Neutral by Terry Trueman
Make Lemonade by Virginia Euwer Wolff

Carryovers to 20*
Federal Car...
Sub Use of...
Net Due (re...
Deductible...

SELF-DEFENSE OF A PERSON

...erson may defend himself/herself or any third person who had a ri...
...ans that are proportionate to the risk threatened. If the response ...
...ponse under this defense, the defendant will be liable. A person cannot s...
...self-defense.

...tion (Modern Trend): Permits the use of force to defend another ...enever th...
...aided person would have the right to self-defense.

...e before you use
...f you are in
...ely.

If faced with deadly force, the majority rule state...
deadly force in self-defense. The modern tren...
your own home, or you cannot retreat safely...

Distinction : Retreat required ...
...nnot do so safely
(I)   ...dwelling
(II)
(III)
(IV)

We the undersigned give permission for our child to participate in the cheerleading program, realizing fully the responsibilities and duties involved. We also accept full responsibility and will not hold the school or its staff accountable for any injuries, damages, losses, or death that may occur at a cheerleading function.

STUDENT'S NAME: ___Ginny Davis___ ☺

GUARDIAN'S SIGNATURE(S): _____

Mom,
please sign
this or I
can't try out!
— Ginny
↘

Ginny,
Cheerleading? maybe you
should join the debate
team instead. You're
much better at arguing
then backflips.

P...
an...

D...

Distinction:
Retreat required before using deadly force unless th...

HEART-HEALTHY CASSEROLE

This is a dish that the whole family will love.

Make your own bread crumbs to make this casserole even more special.

WHILE YOU WERE

Grocery List

we ran out of...

- lentils
- tofu
- spring water
- organic chicken
- dark chocolate
- bok choy
- celery
- brown rice
- soy sauce
- tempeh
- baba ghanoush
- toilet paper
- pita bread
- stain remover
- tampons

(Ginny: What size do you want me to buy you? Also do you need pantiliners? — Mom)

MOM!!!!!!!!!!!!

your hands

ATTENTION, ALL MEMBERS OF THE HOUSEHOLD:

Who is using up all the toilet paper? You kids better not be getting into trouble at Halloween this year or I am shipping you off to an orphanage. (Except for Timmy; I'll send him to the Island of Sodor to hang out with Thomas.)

Sincerely,
The Management

"Family Dinner"

Family Dinner was
my stepfather's big idea.
He read an article that said
it's important to eat dinner
as a family every night
(communication is key).
Bob's on a healthy-eating kick
so he made an organic casserole
(lentils, brown rice, edamame, tofu cheese).
We went around the table
talking about our day.
Henry said that someone
pulled the fire alarm (but it wasn't him).
Timmy said that gerbil pellets
don't taste as bad as you'd think
(he only ate twelve; it was a dare).
I said that I was going to try
out for the cheerleading squad
(they are not bimbos).
Then Mom stood up,
said she felt sick,
and barfed all over the kitchen floor
(she missed the dog).
Bob said that maybe we'll just do
Family Dinner
once a week from now on.

Organic is Awesome! (I'm a vegetarian myself.) —Ms. T.

ATTENTION, ALL MEMBERS OF THE HOUSEHOLD:

I know we are all used to the old "door lock" concept, but here is a simple refresher course for our new alarm system:

1) If you open a door when the alarm is on, you will set off the alarm.
2) The alarm company will call the house, and if you tell them that you can't talk because you are on Level Twelve of your family-friendly video game EVIL TEDDY BEARS, they will call the police.
3) Then the police will come. And the new neighbors will not be charmed. Nor will Bob (who will have to leave work). Or me (who will have to walk out of court).
4) So DO NOT OPEN THE DOOR WHEN THE ALARM IS SET!!!!!

Thank you for your cooperation in this.
Sincerely,
The Management

CONGRATS
TO ALL OUR NEW COUGARS!

Maddie Chan
Breanna Colella
Brittany Colella
Fiona Cushman
Genevieve Davis
Jo Edgehill
Katelyn Epstein
GiGi Hampton
Mary Catherine Kelly
Gabrielle Ortiz
Diana Pancu
Sophie Posse
JulieAnn Savino
Ria Taylor

First practice will be Tuesday, September 29 at 3:00 pm.
Get ready for our Gummi Bear Fund-Raiser to help send
us to Regionals!!

: 29
with
all.

d
om on
attire.
ents!

BULLY

IS VERY SERIOU
TOLERATED ON
ANYONE YOU K
DO NOT HESITA
FRIENDLY GUID
IMMEDIATE ACT
ENSURE EVERY
LIVELIHOOD T

Just Deserves (~~Desserts~~)

My old best friend (~~Mary Catherine Kelly~~)
beat me out
for a lead in ballet last year
(not that she didn't deserve it).
She said mean things
about my older brother
after he got in big trouble
(not that he didn't deserve it)
and made fun of
my new stepfather's
boxer shorts
(not that they didn't deserve it).
It figures that she would
try out for cheer, too,
and make the squad
(not that she doesn't deserve it).
It's just that
I wanted something for
myself without her around
(don't I deserve it?).

THAT'S MY GINNY GIRL!
DON'T LET THEM DROP YOU!
SEE YOU AT
THANKSGIVING.

(THINK THEY'LL LET ME CHEER?)

— GRAMPA JOE
(AKA THE OLD GUY
IN FLORIDA)

FLORIDA
POST CARD

44 CENTS

GENEVIEVE DAVIS
EDEN VALLEY ESTATES
1026 GRASSLANDS VIEW
WOODLAND GLEN, PA
18762

FLORIDA

gr8

Cougar Cheer Schedule

OCTOBER

Saturday 3 Game home
Friday 9 Game away
Saturday 10 County Cheer away
Saturday 17 Game away
Sunday 18 Charity Cheer away
Friday 23 Game away
Saturday 24 Fall Classic Competition away

Ginny
You're going to have
to find some other
girls to carpool with
Bob's got reenactment
and Timmy has soc
Mom

NOVEMBER

Sunday 1 Game home

MAIL
CONTACTS
TASKS

COMPOSE

INBOX (2)
SENT MAIL
DRAFTS (2)
SPAM (45)
TRASH

GINNY'S
HOMEWORK
FRIENDSTUFF
POEMS
VIDEO GAMZ
V VIX'S
KEWT IM CHATS
OLD STUFF ZZZ...

CHAT

Invite, add, search

Carpool 4 Cougars

BACK TO INBOX   SPAM   ARCHIVE   NEXT   FILE IN

Ginny ▶ Cheer Girls

Carpool 4 Cougars

Can anyone carpool with me on the weekends?
My mom says we can take turns.

   —Ginny

◀ REPLY

I wish
my mom could just
be happy for me.
I try to explain that being a cheerleader
is cool now.
You have to be an athlete
and know how to tumble.
You have to be able to
be thrown on the
shoulders of someone else
without getting yourself killed.
It's not like when she was in school,
when all cheerleaders did
was wear tight sweaters
and shake pom-poms.

I wish
my mom could just
be happy for me.
But I guess she's still mad
about not being
picked for a cheerleader.
She joined the debate team instead.

33

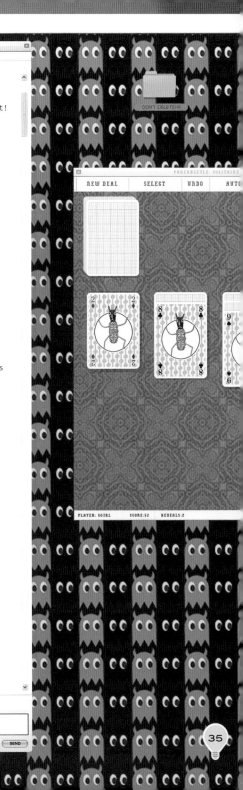

GinnyGirl

OMG mi mom is pregnant! I thought she was jst getting fat!

beckysooboo1

OMG! OMG! She's a grannymom!

GinnyGirl

what's a grannymom?

beckysooboo1

an old mom!

GinnyGirl

She iz pretty old. She's 39!

beckysooboo1

Do u think shez having twins? Or 3lets? I luv all those shows with multiples!

GinnyGirl

omg. I hope not.

beckysooboo1

r you going to have to change diapers?

GinnyGirl

omg. I hope not.

beckysooboo1

You think she'll be like Mary Catherine's mom who was always breastfeeding in public?

GinnyGirl

omg. I hope not.

WRITE   PHOTO   EMOTICON

SEND

35

Grocery List

we ran out of...
- toilet paper
- folic acid
- saltines
- candy for trick-or-treaters
- brown rice
- tofu burgers
- sprouts
- salsa
- avocado
- potato chips
- and Timmy wants chicken nuggets!

-AND HENRY WANTS POTATO CHIPS

JOIN IN THE FRIGHTENING FUN

The Woodland Central Annual *MONSTER MASH!*

Dancing, Pizza, and Costume Prizes

Doors Open at 7pm!

Cost: $5/child

Parents must drop off and pick up.

Costume required. Any child whose costume is deemed inappropriate by chaperone will be sent home.

"Build Your Own Tofu Burger!"

This is a healthy twist on family burger night.
Use fresh toppings like salsa, sprouts, and avocado to add zest!

For extra flavor, marinate the tofu in lemon juice, olive oil, rosemary, and a crushed clove of garlic.

THE BRAVE EATER HEALTHY FOOD FOR COOL PEOPLE

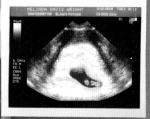

"Buttons"

My stepfather is a Civil War buff.
He likes to visit battlefields
and dress up and take part
in reenactments.
All these grown men
run around fields
shouting and
pretending to die.
Bob says
that everything's
Historically Accurate
right down to the
buttons
on his wool uniform.
It's pretty boring,
not to mention
I didn't know
Civil War soldiers
had camera phones.

*Ha-ha!
Your stepfather
sounds awesome,
Ginny! — Ms. T.*

OMG my mom
barfed in court
in front of the
judge! — G

Ewww!! = 💀
she said it's
the morning
sickness.

did she win?

Nope! (I think
the judge was
grossed out)

me 2!!

She's quitting her job. She sez being
a stay-at-home mom can't be any
harder than being a lawyer.

39

you want to come to Monster Mash with me? -G

Only if you dress as a worm. -B

40

ATTENTION, HOUSEHOLD MEMBERS:

The refrigerator defrosted for some unknown reason last night. All the food was ruined. Please do not put anything in it. The repairman can't get here until next Friday, so we will be ordering in until further notice.

Sincerely,
The Management

HARRY'S BURGER

HOME OF THE
...NIGHT CHEESEBURGER

... ARRY'S BURGER

BURGERS

...urger	5.00
...le Burger	7.50
...oo Burger	8.99
...on Soft French Roll w/Fries	
...nd Slam Burger	9.99
...on Large Bun w/Fries	
...cken Burger	5.25
...0 Island Dressing, Lettuce & Tomato	
...rden Burger	5.99
...yo, Lettuce & Tomato	
...d Burger	5.99
...000 Island Dressing, Lettuce & Tomato	

...DDY PANDA
...THENTIC CHINESE CUISINE

...ULTRY 鸡肉

Sesame Chicken	$6.50
Chicken W. Broccoli	$6.25
...ung-Pao Chicken	$6.50
...picy Chicken	$6.50
...unan Chicken	$6.50
...hicken in Garlic Sauce	$6.50
...neral Tso Chicken	$6.50

猪肉

...Fried Pork Chop W. Black Pepper & Spices	$6.25
...ied Pork Chop W. Honey & Rice Vinegar	$6.25
...W. Broccoli	$6.25
...led Pork in Garlic Sauce	$6.25
...led Pork & Dry Bean Curd Stir Fried	
...nese Thin Celery	$6.25

肉

...Broccoli	$6.75
...teak W. Onion	$6.75
...eef Stir Fried W. Green Hot Pepper	$6.75
...ried W. Scallion in Brown Sauce	$6.75
...eef & Dry Bean Curd W. Chinese Thin Celery	$6.75
...vored Beef	$6.75
...ck of Beef	$6.75

海鲜

...under	$6.95
...nder	$6.95
...weet & Sour Sauce	$6.95
...picy Bean Sauce	$6.95
...ccoli	$6.95
...ster Sauce	$6.95
...ew Nuts	$6.95
...n Pea	$6.95
...hrimp W. Bean Curd in a Casserole	$7.95
...an Curd in a Casserole	$7.95

蔬菜

...Fried W. Bean Curd Sheet & Soy Bean	$5.95
...quash	$5.95
...an W. Garlic	$5.95
...rd W. Vegetables	$5.95
...hef's Special Chili Sauce	$5.95
...tion in Shanghai Style	$6.25
...Wheat Gluten, Snow Peas, Dry Bean Curd	
...uce	$6.25
...Garlic Sauce	$6.25

※ Hot & Spicy

#6 Buffalo Wings 10 pc. With Ranch dressing $7.00

#7 Two tacos/crispy shell, choose from chicken, shredded beef, ground beef, with lettuce, cheese, and Pico de Gallo, small salsa and chips $6.00

#8 Big Quesadilla, cheddar and monterey jack cheese, chicken or steak with guacamole and Pico de Gallo small salsa and chips $8.00

...ING ...BRERO

...to-go
...menu

...ef, steak, chicken, shredded
... verde, with rice/beans, chips

...d Beef or ground beef with

...ak fajita, shredded beef, ground
...it comes with rice, refried or
...sour cream, and guacamole.

...with olives, guacamole, sour

...hicken monterey jack cheese,
...chips $5.00

...R BAMBOO THAI

...ice	4.00	5.00
...emon Sauce	4.00	5.00
...ken		
...auce ♪	3.60	4.60
...ng Onion		
	3.60	4.60
...ken		
...e ♪	4.00	5.00
...Nuts		
...Sauce	3.60	4.60
...ew Nuts	3.60	4.60
...uan Sauce	3.60	4.60
...pple ♪	3.50	4.50
...ean Sauce	3.50	4.50
...oom	3.50	4.50
...auce	3.50	4.50
...le	3.50	4.50
...oots		
	3.50	4.50
...ne	3.50	4.50
	3.50	4.50

BEEF

...♪	3.60	4.60
	3.60	4.60
	3.60	4.60
	3.50	4.50
...uce	3.50	4.50
	3.50	4.50
...e ♪	3.50	4.50
...bles	3.50	4.50
	3.50	4.50

GINNY—
MY EVIIIIIIL
PLAN WORKED!
CHINESE TONIGHT,
PIZZA TOMORROW!
(TOFU BURGERS=
TORTURE BURGERS)
—HENRY

42

Ginny's Big To-Do List

1. ~~Try out for cheer~~
2. ~~Convince Mom to let me bike~~   scooter?
3. ~~Fall in love~~   ~~to school~~
4. Work on art (sketch every day)
5. Save money
6. Look good in family Christmas photo
7. ~~Join Vampire Vixens Den~~
8. Teach Grampa Joe how to email
9. ~~Have a cool Halloween~~
                    ~~costume for once~~

10. Ignore horoscopes!

happiness

44

❥ MOOD:
(dreamy!) :-o

❥ SHARE:
pic / video

❥ RAMBLING THOUGHTS:
I like wormz.

vamp chat

vixen friends:

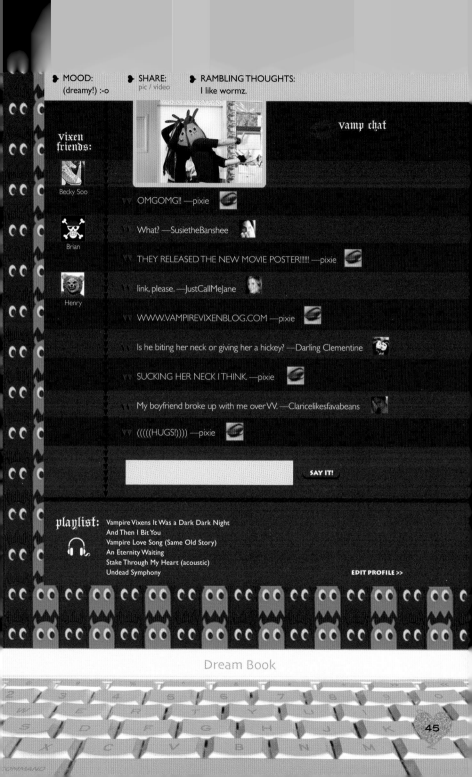

Becky Soo

Brian

Henry

OMGOMG!! —pixie

What? —SusietheBanshee

THEY RELEASED THE NEW MOVIE POSTER!!!!!! —pixie

link, please. —JustCallMeJane

WWW.VAMPIREVIXENBLOG.COM —pixie

Is he biting her neck or giving her a hickey? —Darling Clementine

SUCKING HER NECK I THINK. —pixie

My boyfriend broke up with me over VV. —Claricelikesfavabeans

(((((HUGS!)))) —pixie

SAY IT!

playlist: Vampire Vixens It Was a Dark Dark Night
And Then I Bit You
Vampire Love Song (Same Old Story)
An Eternity Waiting
Stake Through My Heart (acoustic)
Undead Symphony

EDIT PROFILE >>

Dream Book

45

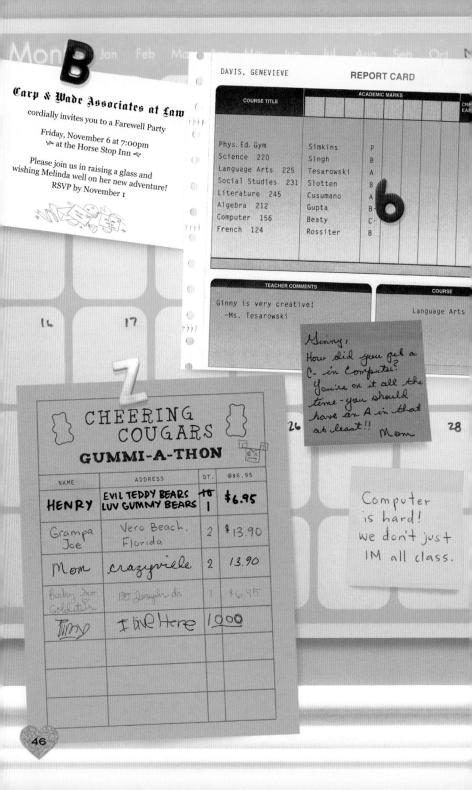

Carp & Wade Associates at Law

cordially invites you to a Farewell Party

Friday, November 6 at 7:00pm
at the Horse Stop Inn

Please join us in raising a glass and
wishing Melinda well on her new adventure!
RSVP by November 1

DAVIS, GENEVIEVE   **REPORT CARD**

COURSE TITLE	ACADEMIC MARKS		
Phys. Ed. Gym	Simkins	P	
Science 220	Singh	B	
Language Arts 225	Tesarowski	A	
Social Studies 231	Slotten	B	
Literature 245	Cusumano	A	
Algebra 212	Gupta	B-	
Computer 156	Beaty	C-	
French 124	Rossiter	B	

TEACHER COMMENTS

Ginny is very creative!
—Ms. Tesarowski

COURSE

Language Arts

Ginny,
How did you get a
C- in Computer?
You're on it all the
time - you should
have an A in that
at least!! Mom

Computer
is hard!
We don't just
IM all class.

CHEERING
COUGARS
GUMMI-A-THON

NAME	ADDRESS	QT.	@$6.95
HENRY	EVIL TEDDY BEARS LUV GUMMY BEARS	~~10~~ 1	$6.95
Grampa Joe	Vero Beach, Florida	2	$13.90
Mom	crazyville	2	13.90
Becky Soo Goldstein	135 Joseph dr	1	$6.95
Timmy	I LIVE HERE	1000	

46

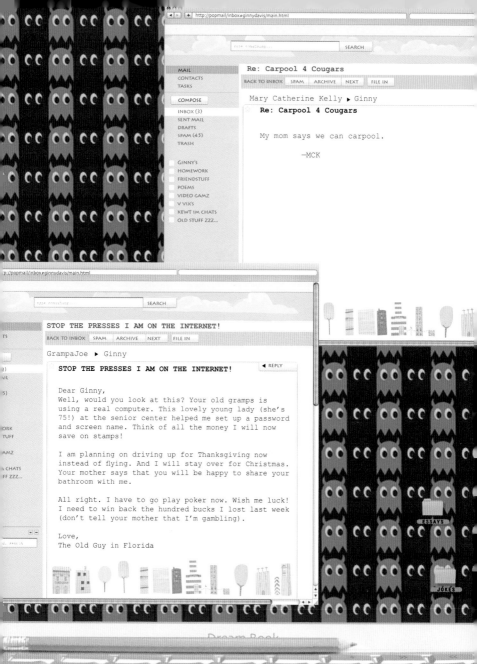

SEARCH

MAIL
CONTACTS
TASKS

COMPOSE

INBOX (3)
SENT MAIL
DRAFTS
SPAM (45)
TRASH

GINNY'S
HOMEWORK
FRIENDSTUFF
POEMS
VIDEO GAMZ
V VIX'S
KEWT IM CHATS
OLD STUFF ZZZ...

Re: Carpool 4 Cougars

BACK TO INBOX   SPAM   ARCHIVE   NEXT   FILE IN

Mary Catherine Kelly ▶ Ginny

Re: Carpool 4 Cougars

My mom says we can carpool.

　　　　　—MCK

SEARCH

STOP THE PRESSES I AM ON THE INTERNET!

BACK TO INBOX   SPAM   ARCHIVE   NEXT   FILE IN

GrampaJoe ▶ Ginny

STOP THE PRESSES I AM ON THE INTERNET!

◀ REPLY

Dear Ginny,
Well, would you look at this? Your old gramps is
using a real computer. This lovely young lady (she's
75!) at the senior center helped me set up a password
and screen name. Think of all the money I will now
save on stamps!

I am planning on driving up for Thanksgiving now
instead of flying. And I will stay over for Christmas.
Your mother says that you will be happy to share your
bathroom with me.

All right. I have to go play poker now. Wish me luck!
I need to win back the hundred bucks I lost last week
(don't tell your mother that I'm gambling).

Love,
The Old Guy in Florida

ESSAYS

JOKES

Dream Book

CHILLERADE
Tropical Punch
100% juice

new txt msg (1) Momcat

**Momcat > ggirl:
I have already taken
away Timmy's trains.**

1 @ 👤   2 abc   3 def
4 ghi   5 jkl   6 mno
7 pqrs   8 tuv   9 wxyz
* + ↑   0 🔒   # 🔔

49

French Lecon

Aller – to go

Present Future
Je vais je irai
To vas to iras
Il va il ira
Nous allons nous irons
Vous allez vous irez
Ils vont ils iront

Do you want to irez to see
the new Vampire Vixens
movie on Saturday with
Brian and me?
My step-Bob's letting
Henry drive us. —G

Wah!
Je fais
babysit. —BB

What does
fais mean?

"I
have to"

Aaah! ;-)

50

txt msg (0)

**ggirl > H:
Henry where r u?**

1@⚏ 2 abc 3 def
4 ghi 5 jkl 6 mno
7 pqrs 8 tuv 9 wxyz
*+⊣ 0⚏⚙ #⚙

51

that was a good movie.
I didn't know Vampires were hot chicks
who wore leather miniskirts.
I thought they were old dead dudes
        named Rudolfo. -B

Told u so. —G

What happened
with your brother?

u don't want
to know.

Yo Science

Vampire Vixens

PLAY FIRST
Multiplex

VAMPIRE VIXENS
Return from
Death Valley

PLAY FIRST
Multiplex

VAMPIRE VIXENS

SATUR...

THEATRE 4
SATURDAY MATINEE

wacky

PLAY FIRST
Multiplex

Screenwide Movie Theaters
Corporate Headquarters/Customer Relations
Wilmington, DE

Henry Davis
Eden Valley Estates
1026 Grasslands View
Woodland Glen, PA 18762

RE: Play First Multiplex

Dear Mr. Davis:

You are hereby banned from Play First Multiplex and from all Screenwide movie theaters. Inappropriate use of a fire extinguisher is a violation of the fire code and a threat to public safety.

If you are discovered on said property, we shall have no recourse but to move forward with criminal charges.

Sincerely,
Katherine Carradine, Esq.

PLEASE
WAKE ME
FOR MEAL

You're lucky Mom's
a lawyer. -G

YOU HAVE NO
SENSE OF HUMOR.
BESIDES, THAT
JERK HAD IT COMING.
HE WOULDN'T GIVE
ME MY
FREE
REFILL.
—H

53

WHILE YOU WE[R]

"T Day" Grocery List

we ran out of.

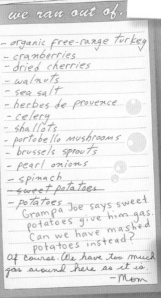

- organic free-range turkey
- cranberries
- dried cherries
- walnuts
- sea salt
- herbes de provence
- celery
- shallots
- portobello mushrooms
- brussels sprouts
- pearl onions
- spinach
- sweet potatoes
- potatoes   Grampa Joe says sweet
   potatoes give him gas.
   Can we have mashed
   potatoes instead?
Of course. We have too much
gas around here as it is
                    —Mom

THE PERFECT THANKSGIVING DINNER

55

"Al's"

I am thankful
for Al's.
The fancy,
high-tech
new oven
in our house
broke and so
the turkey was raw.
Luckily for us,
Al's was open
and delivers.
They even threw
in some free garlic bread
when they heard
what happened.

Yum! I love garlic bread! Sounds like an awesome Thanksgiving to me!
— Ms. I.

French Gender

Masculine = le, un ◎
Feminine = la, une ◉
Examples: hat = le chapeau
house = la maison

This is sooooo stupid.
How is a hat masculine??
-G

Maybe the hat has a beard! —BB

How do you say lol in French?

Want to study 4 the French test with me 2nite?

I have cheer practice.

56

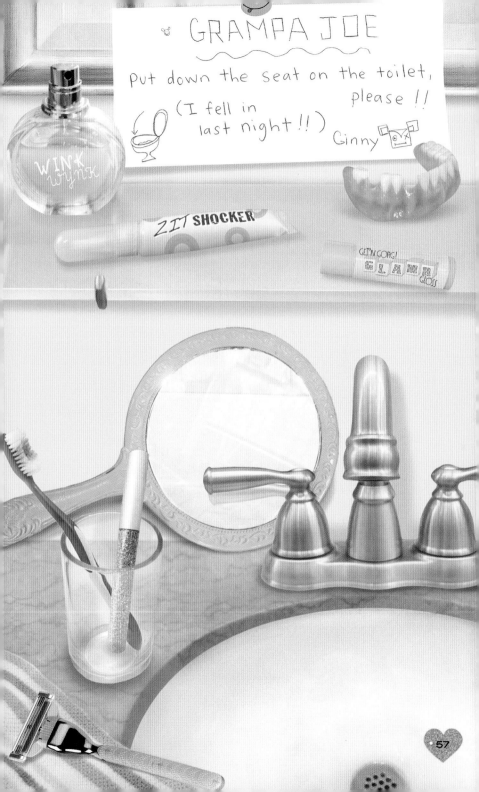

CAUTION

~~Homework~~ CUPCAKE
Zone
BE CAREFUL OF FROSTI...

Name: Genevieve Davis

Class: Social Studies

Assignment: Please discuss the origins of the Revolutionary War.

WAR

It was taxation without representation. They also wanted cupcakes. Lots of cupcakes.

BABY NAMES
(American Revolution Version)

Benedict
Betsy
Cornwallis
Benjamin
Franklin
Nathaniel
George
Paul
Lafayette

BABY NAMES
(Vampire Version)

Buffy
Cordelia
Dracula
Bones
Lestat
Lucretia
Spike
Vampirella
Edward (sparkly!)
Count Chocula (tasty!)

58

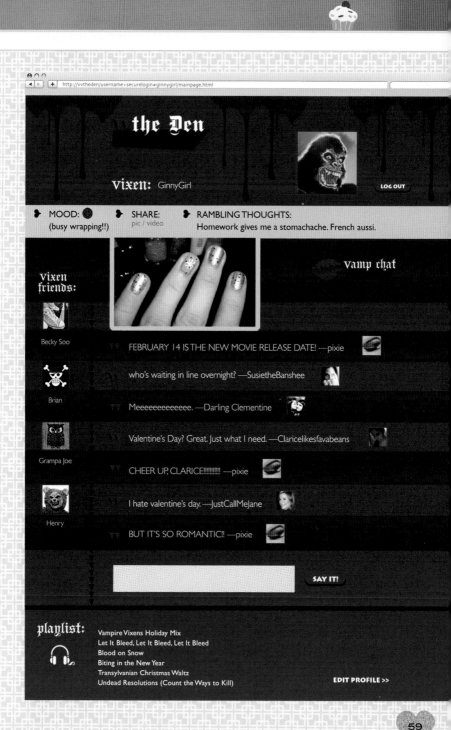

the Den

vixen: GinnyGirl

LOG OUT

➤ MOOD: 😈
(busy wrapping!!)

➤ SHARE:
pic / video

➤ RAMBLING THOUGHTS:
Homework gives me a stomachache. French aussi.

vixen friends:

Becky Soo

Brian

Grampa Joe

Henry

vamp chat

FEBRUARY 14 IS THE NEW MOVIE RELEASE DATE! —pixie

who's waiting in line overnight? —SusietheBanshee

Meeeeeeeeeeeee. —Darling Clementine

Valentine's Day? Great. Just what I need. —Claricelikesfavabeans

CHEER UP, CLARICE!!!!!!!!!!! —pixie

I hate valentine's day. —JustCallMeJane

BUT IT'S SO ROMANTIC!! —pixie

SAY IT!

playlist:

Vampire Vixens Holiday Mix
Let It Bleed, Let It Bleed, Let It Bleed
Blood on Snow
Biting in the New Year
Transylvanian Christmas Waltz
Undead Resolutions (Count the Ways to Kill)

EDIT PROFILE >>

FILL IN THE BLANK

Study hall is _AWESOME_.
Dissecting worms is _AWESOME_.
You think Ginny is _AWESOME_.

I hear there
is going to
be a ski trip
to Vermont
over spring
break. —B

Maybe I
should learn
to ski. —G

No—learn to snowboard!
It's awesome!
(for real/z)

OK!

one cupcake
to rule
them all!

Xmas Shopping List

Mom— maternity shirt
Bob— tofu
Henry— evil teddy bear
Timmy— Thomas the Tank
Grampa Joe— new dentures case
Becky Soo— cell phone case
Brian— worms?

TAKE-HOME TEST — Quest in The Hobbit.

Ginny Davis
Ginny Davis
Ginny Davis

Ginny,
Your mom said you
need some help on
The Hobbit? It's my
favorite book of all
time. Ask me anything.
Bilbob

The Hobbit

Genevieve Davis

Take-Home Test

1. Please discuss the role of The Quest in The Hobbit.
   Is Bilbo a reluctant hero?

2. How do riddles play an important role in
   The Hobbit?

Bilbo must prove that brains (answering riddles)
are more important than brawn (fighting) when
he is confronting Gollum.

3. What does Gollum represent in the human experience?

4. What is the symbolism of The Ring?

ing Date	Transaction Description	Deposits & Interest	Checks & Subtractions	Daily Balance
01	Beginning Balance			$14.00
5	Deposit	+ $20.00		$34.00
	ATM		- $10.00	$24.00
	Deposit	+ $20.00		$44.00
	ATM		- $50.00	- $6.00
	OVERDRAFT FEE		- $15.00	- $21.00
	Ending Balance			- $21.00

un-mistaker

61

NOVEL STUDY: Ginny Davis

Book title: <u>Monsoon Summer</u> by Mitali Perkins

Style of book: Prose

Discuss the narrator:

Jazz is fifteen and lives in California.
She is in love with her best friend.

Discuss the plot:

Jazz and her family travel to India for the
summer to volunteer at an orphanage because
her mom grew up there. Everything is totally
different in India.

Your thoughts:

I could relate to Jazz because I think it would
be hard to live in a new place, too. Also, Jazz's
relationship with her mom reminded me of my
mom. (Although my mom is bossier than Jazz's mom.)
I think it's because she's a lawyer and she's used
to arguing with people all day.

Would you recommend this book:

yes! (I already gave it to Becky Soo.)

I THOUGHT YOU WOULD ENJOY THIS ONE!

— Mr. Cusumano

Ginny's Christmas List

- my own credit card
  G: You can dream
            — Mom

- new cell phone
    with extended
       keyboard

- snowboarding
  jacket and pants

- gloves / hat
   goggles too

Why is this incomplete ????

I had a late game to
cheer for that night!
And nobody speaks
French around here
anyway!   — Ginny

<u>Incomplete</u>

Name: Je'nevieve

Conjugate the following verbs in present, future,
and imperfect tenses using first person singular.

être:

aller: Je vais, J'irai, J'allais

venir:

lire:

partir: Je parti,

rire: Je ri

suivre:

ouvrir:

dire: Je dit,

aimer: J'aime, J'aimerai

62

SHIP TO: Henry Davis

Eden Valley Estates
1026 Grasslands View
Woodland Glen, PA
18762

NEXT-DAY SHIPPING
SATISFACTION GUARANTEED!

SHIP TO: Henry Davis
Eden Valley Estates
1026 Grasslands View
Woodland Glen, PA
18762

NEXT-DAY SHIPPING
SATISFACTION GUARANTEED!

GAME OVER

❤❤❤❤❤❤❤❤❤❤❤

EVIL TEDDY BEARS
YOU BEAT THE STUFFING OUT OF ME!

HIGH SCORES

```
1 Ginnybear 3200
2 Ginnybear 3175
3 Ginnybear 3005
4 Ginnybear 2250
5 Ginnybear 2200
6 Ginnybear 2000
7 Henry     1950
```

65

Assignment: Write a poem about the holiday season. Enjoy winter break!

"Scrooge"

My stepfather
got laid off
a week before
Christmas.
No notice.
No severance.
No nothing.
What kind of person
does this?
I bet his name is
Scrooge.

Sorry to hear this!
Have an awesome
winter break! See
you in the New Year!
— Ms. T.

Happy holidays from Ms. T.

Worm
guy

Who keeps decapitating the gingerbread men? **NOT ME** Not me! I ONLY ATE ONE HEAD

Main Line Cars
SPECIALIZING IN FOREIGN & EXOTIC CARS

ervice Department Estimate

eplace shifter	
place rear suspension	$1,000.00
or	$850.00
al	$800.00
This is an estimate only.	$2,650.00

If your grades slip any more, my little poet, you're off the cheer squad.
— Mom
P.S. Bob agrees with me.

REPORT CA

DAVIS, GENEVIEVE

ACADEMIC MA

COURSE TITLE

Phys. Ed. Gym
Science 220
Language Arts 225
Social Studies 231
Literature 245
Algebra 212
Computer 156
French 124

Simkins
Singh
Tesarowski
Slotten
Cusumano
Gupta
Beaty
Rossiter

P
B-
A-
B
B
C+
C-
B

COURSE

TEACHER COMMENTS

Language Arts

Ginny is a wonderful poet! —Ms. Tesarowski

Parent's

THE **WORMERY**
WORM HOTEL

Make your own amazing Sanctuary for Worms!

TONS OF

DESIGN YOUR OW
WITH FUN STICKER

ENDLESS HOURS OF
WORM - WATCHING!

JOLLY
CHRISTMAS
To You

BUY SOME SOCKS!
(OR A SNOWBOARD
JACKET!)

GRAMPA
JOE

to : G

RETIREMENT COMMUNITY

12/2

GINNY DAVIS $5
THREE HUNDRED

JOE MASELL

68

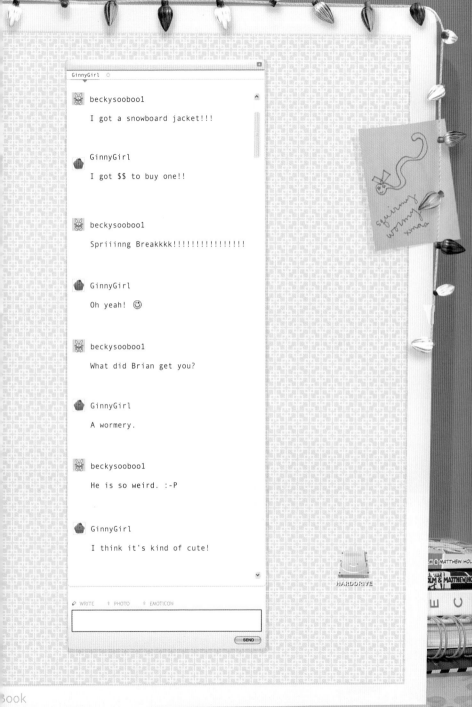

beckysooboo1
I got a snowboard jacket!!!

GinnyGirl
I got $$ to buy one!!

beckysooboo1
Spriiinng Breakkkk!!!!!!!!!!!!!!!!

GinnyGirl
Oh yeah! 😊

beckysooboo1
What did Brian get you?

GinnyGirl
A wormery.

beckysooboo1
He is so weird. :-P

GinnyGirl
I think it's kind of cute!

✎ WRITE   ⚲ PHOTO   ☺ EMOTICON

SEND

HARDDRIVE

Book

G —

I GOT THE NEW EVIL TEDDY
BEARS GAME! EVIL TEDDY BEARS
VS. THE PLASTIC BABY DOLLS!
(GUARANTEED TO GIVE YOU
NIGHTMARES FOR WEEKS OR YOUR
MONEY BACK!)
P.S. MEET ME IN MY ROOM!
— H

NO
WORM
murderers
ALLOWED!
THIS MEANS YOU, TIMMY!!!

71

GRAMPA JOE'S NEW YEAR'S EVE

P O K E R
A T H O N

You are invited to the first-ever
"Grampa Joe's Nacho Supreme Poker-a-thon"!

A penny a chip! • Winner takes all tortillas! • Bring your spiciest salsa!

$10

5

Guest List
Grampa Joe
Ginny
Henry
Becky Soo   Brian

Henry's weird
friend Samson

Ginny's "New" New Year To-Do List!

1. Convince Mom to let me go on ski trip
2. Work on art (sketch every day)
3. Save money
4. Get to Regionals for cheer!
5. Have a big birthday party somewhere cool (not at home)
6. See Vampire Vixens in concert!
7. Get steel lock on door to keep Timmy out
8. Avoid nachos
9. Ignore horoscopes
10. Stop making lists

HAVE A GOOD WEEK BACK IN THE SALT MINES. I'LL WAVE TO YOU WHEN I FLY OVER YOUR SCHOOL.
LOVE, GRAMPA JOE
(AKA THE OLD GUY IN FLORIDA)
P.S. IF YOU FIND MY DENTURES, PLEASE MAIL THEM TO ME!!

✚ URGENT CARE

Acct: A0903700390
PATIENT:
DAVIS, GENEVIE...

PATIENT DISCHARGE   DATE JANUARY 1   ☐ Home Health ☐ Psych ☐ Rehab ☐ SNF

Discharge: ☒ Home or Other Facility: ☐ Home Health

COMPLAINT: nausea, diarrhea

Patient claims to have eaten a lot of nachos with very spicy salsa. Possible gastroenteritis. Recommend follow-up with Primary Care Physician for further blood work.

Pain Management Plan: _____
Instructions: ☐ Incision Wound Care ☐ Symptom/Disease

You are invited to a
BABY SHOWER!

For: Melinda

When: February 25, 3pm,
Jill Schorr's House

622-6754 for RSVP

WHILE YOU WERE

BABY NAME POOL

we ran out of...

Thomas (Timmy)
Dracula (me)
Satan's Little Spawn
(Henry)
Maxwell (Becky Soo)
Joseph (Grampa Joe)
Lincoln (Bob)
Al (Joey, the delivery
guy from Al's Pizza)

fifi the
fetus

☐ URGENT

6

1   2   3

8

15

23
Ginny's
Bday!

24

V DAY

SPRING BREAK SKI TRIP
TO VERMONT

Cost per student $400

Includes:
- 3 nights accommodations
- snowboard/ski rental
- lift tickets
- round-trip bus transportation
- 3 meals/day
- $50 nonrefundable deposit

Balance due one week prior to trip.
Please note: Lessons not included.
Lessons are on a group basis ($50/hour).

REMINDER
REMINDER   SECOND NOTICE

6400 6240 XC RP 02 0006659 07290IY   01

Internet Service

	Quantity	A
Monthly Internet Service		
HIGH SPEED INTERNET	1	
BUNDLED SAVINGS PAK	1	-

Cable Service

	Quantity	Am
Monthly Cable Service		
LIMITED BASIC	1	
EXPANDED SERVICE	1	19
DIGITAL SERVICE/DIGITAL GATEWAY	1	27
HD DIGITAL RECEIVER(S)	1	9
Monthly Cable Service	1	5
		$62

74

It's a Bouncing Baby . . . Boy!

WE WELCOME THE NEWEST MEMBER OF THE FAMILY.

BALLOU DAVIS-WRIGHT

BORN FEBRUARY 12
4 LBS., 3 OZ.
17 INCHES

"Ballou"

Ballou

is the name of my new baby brother.
Sullivan Ballou was a Union soldier
who fought in
the First Battle of Bull Run.
His leg got amputated and then he died.
Talk about unlucky.
But he wrote a famous letter
to his wife about democracy and so
Bob thinks he's the greatest,
which is why he wanted
to name the baby Ballou.
Everybody agrees that
it's pretty unique
except Grampa Joe,
who says that
Ballou
is the dumbest name he's ever heard
and that the kid's gonna be
fighting off bullies
for the rest of his life.

excellent

What an
awesome name!
Congrats!
— Ms. T.

"I have no misgivings about, or lack of confidence
in the cause in which I am engaged, and my courage
does not halt or falter. I know how strongly American
Civilization now leans on the triumph of the Government
and how great a debt we owe to those who went before
us through the blood and sufferings of the Revolution."
—Major Sullivan Ballou

- Brian

LOVE

HAPPY
VALENTINE'S
DAY TO MY
BELOVED
SISTER.
GAG!

FOR YOU

U-R COOL

Queen OF HEARTS

TO MY

ROSES ARE RED,
LILIES ARE WHITE,
IF YOU COME TO FLORIDA
FOR SPRING BREAK,
WE'LL HAVE EARLY-BIRD
DINNER EVERY NIGHT!
—GRAMPA JOE
(AKA THE OLD GUY IN FLORIDA)

-B

Gimy

Timmy

BE GOOD

ATTENTION, ALL HOUSEHOLD MEMBERS:

WASH YOUR HANDS & USE THE HAND SANITIZER!! (Ballou is at risk for RSV since he is premature, so please be careful around him.) And PLEASE put poopy diapers in the diaper pail immediately! Do not leave them sitting around!! Otherwise, Hoover will get into them.

Sincerely,
The Management

Grocery List
we ran out of...
- diapers
- wipes
- A+D cream
- pasta
- bread
- milk
- tummy tablets

☐ URGENT

Smart
SELLS Homes
SOLD
Susana Smart
REALTOR
"#1 in Homes Sold in the County!"
susanasmart@smartsellshomes.com

ESTHA-CARE LTD. - EXPLANATION OF BENEFITS

Patient name: Ballou Davis-Wright
ID number: 3548269
Group number: 5543

Physician: Woodland Regional Hospital
Service: NICU/Pediatric Group Care
Charge submitted: $21,100.00

Charge covered: $16,880.00

Your responsibility: $4,220.00
Itemization below.

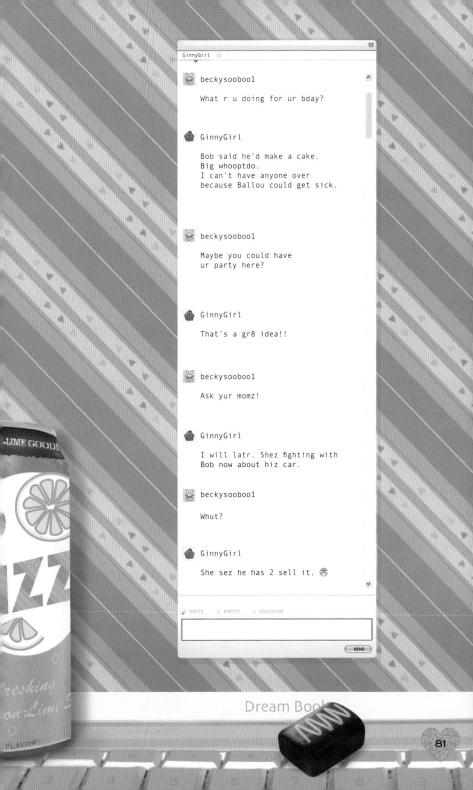

83

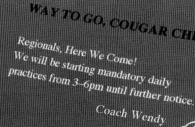

IMPORTANT RULES FOR FETAL PIGS DISSECTION

- Always wear safety gloves, goggles, and apron.
- The preservative is very harmful. Use the eyewash
  IMMEDIATELY if you splash preservative in your eye accidentally.
- Use care with dissection instruments. These are not toys.
- No horseplay whatsoever.

  Should we call him Porky or Babe? —B

- *Treat the pig with respect.*

  I think it's a "her." —G

- *Finally:* THE PIG STAYS IN THE ROOM! Any student discovered
  violating this rule will receive an automatic failure for the course.

What about Charlotte from that kid book?

Charlotte was the spider.

85

Poetry Friday!

Assignment: Write a poem using one of your senses (taste/touch/hear/sight/smell).

"Baby Smells"

I've noticed that there
are a lot of smells
when babies are around.
Some stinky (like diapers).
Some gross (like spit-up).
Some weird
(like organic diaper cream).
But sometimes,
like when Ballou is warm
and sleeping in my arms,
he smells like everything
that's right in the world
(like love and purring kittens
and rainbows).
And it's so sweet and soothing
that I don't mind having baby
smells around.

Oh, I love how babies smell, too!
Especially their cute little heads!
You just want to eat them up!
— Ms. T.

My Ballou

Author study HELP!!!!!!!!!!! PLEASE ANSWER!!!!!!!!!!!!

BACK TO INBOX | SPAM | ARCHIVE | NEXT | FILE IN

Ginny ▶ Kirby Larson

Author study HELP!!!!!!!!!!! PLEASE ANSWER!!!!!!!!!!!!

Dear Ms. Larson,
My name is Ginny and I am in 8th Grade and I have an
Author Study due on you tomorrow. Would it be okay if
I ask you a few questions?

1. Where do you live? When is your birthday?
2. What other books have you written?
3. What is the main theme of Hattie Big Sky?
4. How does the setting in Hattie Big Sky influence the
story?
5. Where do you get your ideas?
6. Can you give me a brief biography of your life?
(Just the big stuff is fine.)
7. Do you have kids? You look pretty young.

Anything else you can think of?

Sincerely,
Ginny Davis

P.S. Can u please email me back soon because
I have to go to bed? Thanks! ☺

FOR SALE

Smart
SELLS
Homes

Price Reduced for Quick Sale!
Call Susana Smart
555-7693

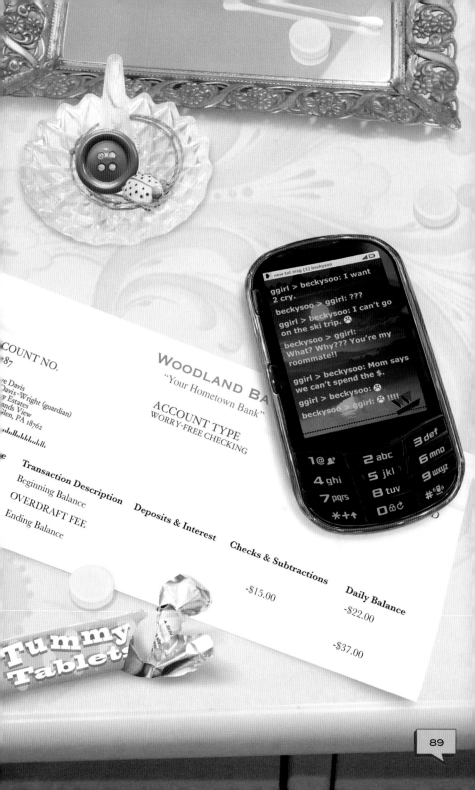

"Spring Broke"

It seems like
everyone
is going somewhere for
spring break.
Becky Soo is going to Vermont,
Zoe Yang
is going to New York City,
and
Dan Kozlov
is going to Disney.
But I'm not going
anywhere
b
e
c
a
u
s
e
we are
broke.

I'm staying at home, too, Ginny! I'm calling it a "staycation." — Ms. T.

Poetry Friday!

Assignment: Write a poem about spring break.

http://popmail/inbox#ginnydavis/main.html

SEARCH

type something...

RE: Carpool

BACK TO INBOX   SPAM   ARCHIVE   NEXT   FILE IN

MAIL
CONTACTS
TASKS

COMPOSE

INBOX
SENT MAIL
DRAFTS
SPAM (45)
TRASH

GINNY'S
HOMEWORK
FRIENDSTUFF
POEMS
VIDEO GAMZ
V VIX'S
KEWT IM CHATS
OLD STUFF ZZZ...

CHAT

invite, add, search

Ginny ▶ Mary Catherine Kelly

RE: Carpool

We sold one of our cars, so we probably wont be able 2
carpool so much now. Can I get a ride with you still?

—Ginny

RE: Re: Carpool

My mom said sure. BTW, I'm not going anywhere for
spring break either. Want 2 hang out?

—MCK   ◀ REPLY

RE: Re: Re: Carpool

Okay.
—G

92

DAVIS, GENEVIEVE

REPORT C

COURSE TITLE

ACADEMIC MARKS

Phys. Ed. Gym 220
Science 220
Language Arts 225
Social Studies 231
Literature 245
Algebra 212
Computer 156
French 124

Simkins   P
Singh   C
Tesarowski   B
Slotten   C
Cusumano   C+
Gupta   C
Beaty   C-
Rossiter   C

TEACHER COMMENTS

I am concerned about Ginny's performance this
quarter. She also seems very tired in class.
—Ms. Tesarowski

Language Arts   COURSE

Parent's Signature

YOU WANT ME
TO DO MOM'S
OR BOB'S
SIGNATURE?
—H

Bob's.
-G

93

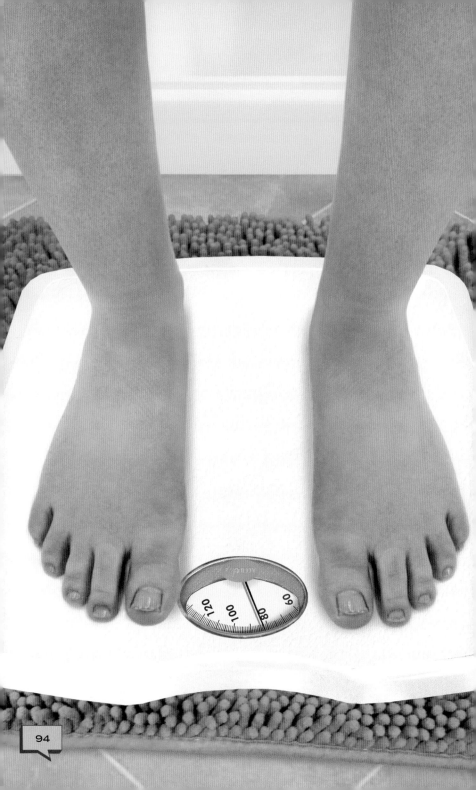

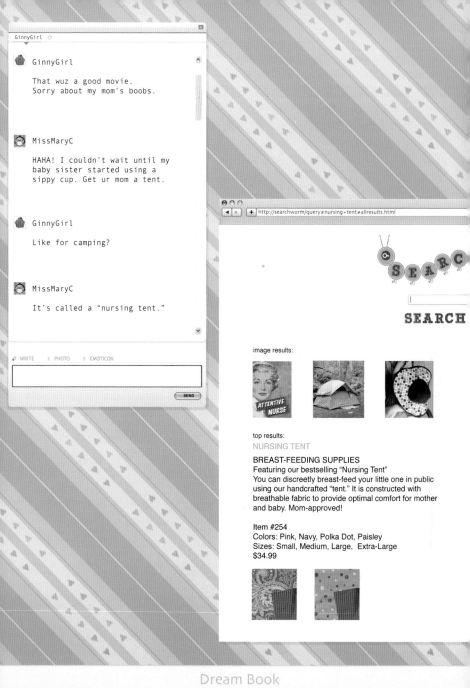

GinnyGirl

GinnyGirl

That wuz a good movie.
Sorry about my mom's boobs.

MissMaryC

HAHA! I couldn't wait until my
baby sister started using a
sippy cup. Get ur mom a tent.

GinnyGirl

Like for camping?

MissMaryC

It's called a "nursing tent."

✏ WRITE   🖼 PHOTO   😊 EMOTICON

SEND

http://searchworm/query#nursing+tent#allresults.html

SEARCH

SEARCH

image results:

ATTENTIVE NURSE

top results:
NURSING TENT

BREAST-FEEDING SUPPLIES
Featuring our bestselling "Nursing Tent"
You can discreetly breast-feed your little one in public
using our handcrafted "tent." It is constructed with
breathable fabric to provide optimal comfort for mother
and baby. Mom-approved!

Item #254
Colors: Pink, Navy, Polka Dot, Paisley
Sizes: Small, Medium, Large, Extra-Large
$34.99

Dream Book

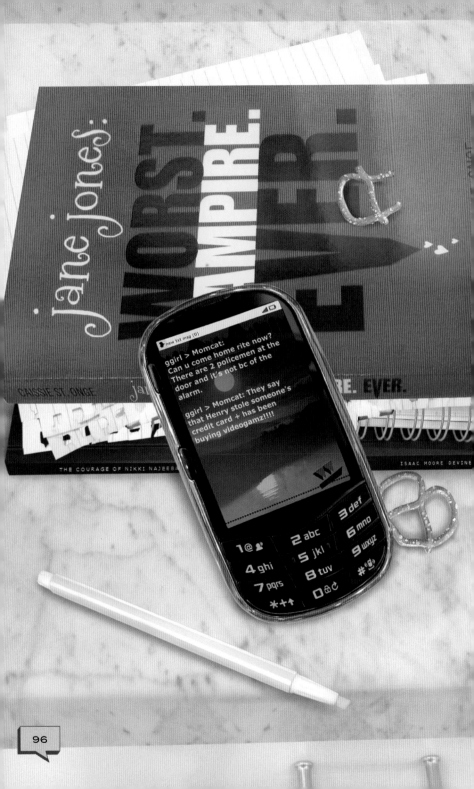

Dear <u>GENEVIEVE DAVIS</u> ,

As per page 10 of the Student Handbook, cell phones are not permitted on school property. I have confiscated the cell phone until a parent or guardian comes into the school to meet with me.

Mrs. MacGillicuty
Mrs. MacGillicuty
Principal

PISCES

LIFE JUST KEEPS GETTING BETTER AND BETTER FOR YOU, PISCES.

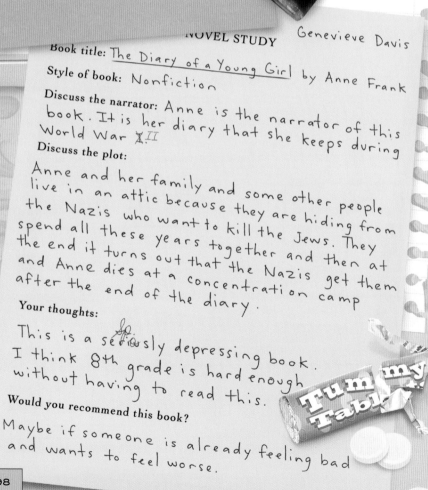

Genevieve Davis

NOVEL STUDY

Book title: <u>The Diary of a Young Girl</u> by Anne Frank

Style of book: Nonfiction

Discuss the narrator: Anne is the narrator of this book. It is her diary that she keeps during World War XII

Discuss the plot:

Anne and her family and some other people live in an attic because they are hiding from the Nazis who want to kill the Jews. They spend all these years together and then at the end it turns out that the Nazis get them and Anne dies at a concentration camp after the end of the diary.

Your thoughts:

This is a seriously depressing book. I think 8th grade is hard enough without having to read this.

Would you recommend this book?

Maybe if someone is already feeling bad and wants to feel worse.

Patient name: Ballou Davis-Wright
ID number: 3548269
number: 5543

Physician: Woodland Regional Hospital
Service: Emergency Department
Charge submitted: $1,375.00

"Bad Luck Insurance"

I know there's life insurance
(for when people die)
and auto insurance
(for when people crash cars)
and health insurance
(for when people get sick).
But what about Bad Luck Insurance
(for when everything goes wrong)?
Like Bob getting laid off.
And Ballou being born too soon.
And Henry being stupid.
I know a lot of people
who would buy Bad Luck Insurance.
Maybe Bob could even sell it.
Because someone around here needs
a job.

Sounds like you are going through a
tough time, Ginny. If you ever want
to talk, my door is always open.
— Ms. T.

Poetry Friday!
assignment: Write a poem about something that's on your mind.

JUVENILE COURT SUMMONS
From the Deputy Clerk of the Juvenile Court

FORM NO. JC 14	COUNTY COURT OF Woodland Glen, PA	CASE NO. 45673

OFFICIAL NOTICE TO:
Melinda Davis-Wright, guardian of the child HENRY DAVIS
residing at Eden Valley Estates, 1026 Grasslands View, Woodland Glen, PA 18762
is hereby summoned to appear in Juvenile Court at
9:30am on APRIL 7 in room 207B   regarding case number 45673.
If you fail to appear, you may be held in contempt of court.

the Den

vixen: GinnyGirl

LOG O[...]

● MOOD: ● SHARE: pic / video   ● RAMBLING THOUGHTS: my stomach is killing me

vixen friends: vamp chat

Becky Soo

Brian

Grampa Joe

I HEAR THEY ARE CASTING SOON! —pixie

They better cast someone who is a good kisser. —Claricelikesfavabeans[...]

THEY SHOULD WAIT UNTIL THEY ARE MARRIED. —pixie

Why??? She's been dead for two hundred years!!! —Claricelikesfavabean[...]

TRUE LOVE IS WORTH WAITING FOR! —pixie

Do you think she has really bad breath from being dead for soooo long[...] —SusietheBanshee

SHE'S NOT DEAD. SHE'S UNDEAD! THERE'S A DIFFERENCE! —pixi[...]

STOP USING ALL CAPS, PIXIE! U R DRIVING ME NUTZ! —GinnyGir[...]

>sorry.< —pixie

SAY IT!

playlist: Vampire Vixens Life After Death Sound Track
Life Sux
Kill Me Now (I'll Still Come Back to Life)
Heartdrainer
I'd Rather Be Dead than Undead
Cold as Ice
Stake Through My Heart

EDIT [...]

"A Good Reason"

My mom's not much of a crier.
She says the only reason to cry
is if things are totally hopeless.
She didn't cry
when Bob got laid off
a week before Christmas.
She didn't cry
when the house was put up for sale
because we couldn't pay the mortgage.
She didn't cry when Henry got arrested
for the credit card scam.
She didn't even cry
when Ballou couldn't breathe
and had to go to the emergency room
in the middle of the night.
But last week,
when Bob came home
and told her for the tenth time
that he didn't get the job,
my mom went into the bathroom
and locked the door and
cried and cried and cried.
And then I started crying, too.

PISCES

Look on the sunny side, Pisces!

ATTENTION,
COUGARS!

The bus will leave for
Regionals promptly at 6am!

Go, Cougars!

1. Bee~
2. Bees~
   drone~
3. Bees~
   necta~
4. Bees li~

HONORS SOCIE

We will be meeting in the
after school from 3pm to
to discuss future endeavo
brainstorming and as alwa

It's
Bee
week!

EMERGENCY ROOM REPORT

LAST NAME: DAVIS	FIRST: GENEVIEVE	MI: N/A		SEX: F

STREET ADDRESS: 1026 GRASSLANDS VIEW	CITY/TOWN: WOODLAND GLEN	STATE: PA	18762

INSURANCE COMPANY NAME: ESTHA-CARE LTD.	POLICY NUMBER: 5543

SYMPTOMS:

Acute dehydration and diarrhea. Fever of 103. Low bp.
Admitted after fainting at cheerleading competition.

HISTORY:

Patient complaint of chronic diarrhea, weight loss, fatigue,
blood in stool. Admitted for observation, rehydration, and
blood workup.

DIAGNOSIS:

Possible irritable bowel syndrome.
Recommend follow-up with GI.

ELL
ELL
ON — Mrs T.

THOUGHT YOU
MIGHT ENJOY THIS!
— MR. C

make lemonade

VIRGINIA EUWER WOLFF

GET UNSICK SOON

$10

Vampire Vixens

Get well or we
will suck your
blood!

Becky Joo

Feel
Better!
**COUGAR
CHEER**
sending you some
Love

Poker Blitz
Ginny — 2
Raquel the Aide — 3
Manny the Nurse — 6
Grampa Joe — 7

Hey C,
do you think we can sneak into the morgue and
dissect a person? I bet they have bodies just
lying around!
— B
P.S. Your grandfather is
Awesome!

$2

NURSE

http://www.iamthesearchworm.net

SEARCH WORM

| ulcerative colitis | 🔍 ▾ |

SEARCH WORM

Search Results (1–10)
see more results...

ULCERATIVE COLITIS

Ulcerative Colitis (UC) is the inflammation of the large intestine.

Symptoms
weight loss
fatigue
abdominal pain and cramping
frequent diarrhea
bloody stools
fever
loss of appetite
anemia

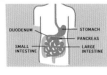

Tests
Sigmoidoscopy or colonoscopy with biopsy

Treatment
Treatment is three-pronged:
Acute inflammation—corticosteroids and hospitalization.
Decrease frequency of flare-ups—anti-inflammatories: 5-aminosalicylates and immunomodulators.
In extreme cases, the colon is surgically removed.

Prognosis
UC is a chronic disease with periods of remission and flare-ups. Stress may exacerbate symptoms.
UC heightens risk of colon cancer.

ESSAYS

⏰ REMINDER!

TUESDAY 10:30
APPOINTMENT WITH DR. KHAN

OKAY

TTT
TEEN TUMMY TRAUMAS
SUPPORT NETWORK
* * *

gab about gluten on
our sister website
GLU
• TEENS

Newly diagnosed?
Tell your story!

I was just diagnosed with ulcerative colitis and besides being completely grossed out that total strangers are talking about my colon and other parts of my body that I have seen in a fetal pig, I am scared about how to tell my friends the real reason why I am in the bathroom all the time and that I can't eat my favorite foods anymore like ice cream or French fries because I have cut all dairy and fatty foods from my diet because they make me so sick.

—GinnyGirl

Hey, GinnyGirl—
It sucks but it could b worse! I have Crohn's and had 2 have some of my intestines removed. Tell ur friends. They'll be kewl.
>If they're real friends.<   —Squirrelly

GinnyGirl,
Wait till you discover rice milk. My mom makes a mean rice milkshake!

        —BenThereDoneThat

GinnyGirl—
Once u start taking the medicine you will feel so much better trust me and try 2 eat lots of small meals.

                              —SevenofTwenty

yo to the yo, ginnygirl,
I call it my "Colin" instead of my "Colon." Too bad I can't break up with it!

                    —Babey

LOL! Colin!

—GinnyGirl

that's one way of getting out of dissecting the pig.

I'd rather be dissecting —B than dissected. —G

P.S. I saved you the tail.

P.S. I saved you a piece of my colon.

Really????

No. ☺ But I do have digital photos from the colonoscopy.

AWESOME!!!!

RICE MAKER

just
POUR &
PRESS!
wow!

For: Ginny
From:
Becky Soo

ATTENTION, ALL HOUSEHOLD MEMBERS:

I will be gone from Monday until Saturday morning. I will be in L.A. from Mon.– Wed., then San Diego Thurs.–Fri.

In my absence, DO NOT:
—Lose the dog
—Lose Timmy
—Lose Ballou
—Forget to empty the diaper pail
—Call me on my cell unless someone is dying.
These are job interviews, people!

REMEMBER:
1) Ginny: Take your medicine.
2) Bob: There is breast milk in the deep freeze.
3) Henry: Do not be late for your community service at the homeless shelter.

Sincerely,
The Management

Genevieve Davis

NOVEL STUDY

Book title: Make Lemonade by Virginia Euwer Wolff

Style of book: Poetry

Discuss the narrator:
La Vaughn is the narrator of this book. She is a very interesting girl.

Discuss the plot:
La Vaughn wants to go to College so she gets a job as a babysitter for a girl named Jolly. Jolly has two kids named Jeremy and Jilly and is poor so La Vaughn babysits for free which is never a good idea, because if you babysit for free the kids are always worse in my opinion. My little brother Timmy is always much better behaved when Mom is paying a real babysitter and not me.

Your thoughts:
I liked that this is written in a poetry style. I didn't know poems could tell a story. Also, I've been getting a lot of lemons lately, so maybe I should try and make some lemonade.

Would you recommend this book?
I wish there was a sequel.

EXCELLENT NOVEL STUDY! THERE ARE TWO SEQUELS.
— MR. CUSUMANO

WHILE YOU WER

Grocery List
we ran out of...

- rice
- rice milk
- rice puffs
- formula
- wipes

☐ URGEN

type something...   SEARCH

MAIL
CONTACTS

RE: :)

Ginny ▶ Mary Catherine Kelly

RE: :)
RE: Re: :)
RE: Re: Re: :)
RE: Re: Re: Re: :)

HA!

—G

beckysooboo1

OMG!!! VV is coming 2
town!!!!!!!!!!!!!!!!!!!!!!!!!!!!!!!

WRITE   PHOTO   EMOTICON

SEND

SuperMom

Is the house still standing?

WRITE   PHOTO   EMOTICON

SEND

GrampaJoe

I got new dentures! I'm having
steak for dinner!

WRITE   PHOTO   EMOTICON

SEND

Henry

2 hours down, 38 to go!
Those homeless kids beat me at
Evil Teddy Bears.

WRITE   PHOTO   EMOTICON

SEND

Dream Book

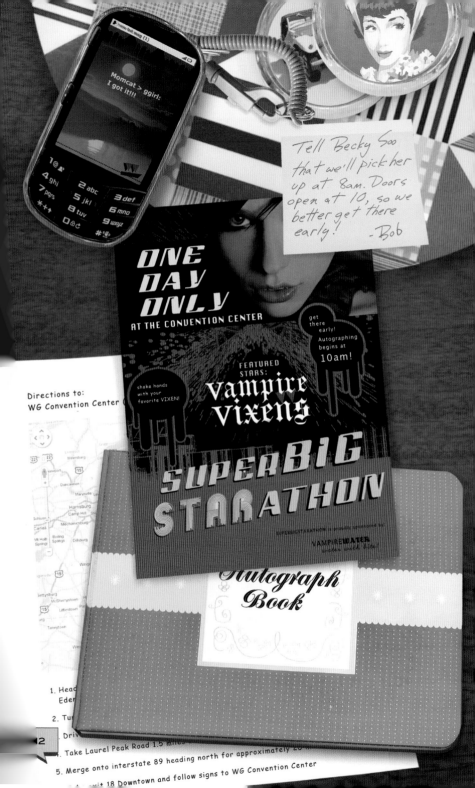

But if you move to California, you will miss these AWESOME tofu tacos!! —Brian

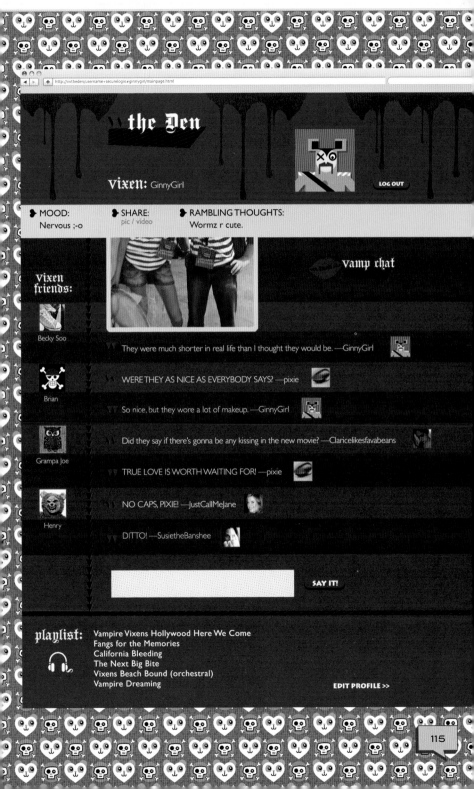

the Den

vixen: GinnyGirl

LOG OUT

MOOD:
Nervous ;-o

SHARE:
pic / video

RAMBLING THOUGHTS:
Wormz r cute.

vamp chat

vixen friends:

Becky Soo

Brian

Grampa Joe

Henry

They were much shorter in real life than I thought they would be. —GinnyGirl

WERE THEY AS NICE AS EVERYBODY SAYS? —pixie

So nice, but they wore a lot of makeup. —GinnyGirl

Did they say if there's gonna be any kissing in the new movie? —Claricelikesfavabeans

TRUE LOVE IS WORTH WAITING FOR! —pixie

NO CAPS, PIXIE! —JustCallMeJane

DITTO! —SusietheBanshee

SAY IT!

playlist:
Vampire Vixens Hollywood Here We Come
Fangs for the Memories
California Bleeding
The Next Big Bite
Vixens Beach Bound (orchestral)
Vampire Dreaming

EDIT PROFILE >>

Poetry Friday

Assignment: Write a poem about something you are looking forward to!

" 2,532 Miles "

It's 2,532 miles
from Pennsylvania to
California.
That's 2,532 miles
from my best friend
(and my worm guy)
and the only place
I have ever lived.
Mom got a job at a big law firm,
and Bob is going to be a SAHD
(stay-at-home dad).
Grampa Joe is going to help
us drive out.
He says we'll make it
an adventure, maybe even
stop in Vegas and do some real
gambling
(we won't tell Mom).
It's like everybody can
breathe again (including me).
I know it's for the best.
But still, it's 2,532 miles.

As you may have guessed, I am
from Southern California myself.
You will love it! It is beyond awesome.
And be sure to rent "Valley Girl" on
DVD — although people don't really
talk like that anymore. Sorry
you'll miss the last two
months of school!
— Ms. T.

116

SEARCH

pink sweater?

MAIL
CONTACTS
TASKS

COMPOSE

INBOX (1)
SENT MAIL
DRAFTS
SPAM (122)
TRASH

GINNY'S
HOMEWORK
FRIENDSTUFF
POEMS
VIDEO GAMZ
V VIX'S
KEWT IM CHATS

Mary Catherine Kelly ▶ Ginny

pink sweater?

I found a pink sweater in the back of my
closet. (I think I borrowed it from you
a long time ago maybe. Sorry.)

RE: pink sweater?

You can keep it!
It looked cuter on you than me anyway. ☺

SEARCH

RE: Author study HELP!!!!!!!!!!! PLEASE ANSWER!!!!!!!!!!!!!!

MAIL
CONTACTS
TASKS

COMPOSE

INBOX (1)
SENT MAIL
DRAFTS
SPAM (122)
TRASH

GINNY'S
HOMEWORK
FRIENDSTUFF
POEMS
VIDEO GAMZ
V VIX'S
KEWT IM CHATS
OLD STUFF ZZZ...

CHAT

Kirby's Desk ▶ Ginny

RE: Author study HELP!!!!!!!!!!! PLEASE ANSWER!!!!!!!!!!!!!!   ◀ REPLY

Dear Ginny,
I do love to hear from readers; thanks for getting in touch. Since you are in a bind, I will
do my best to answer your questions.

1. I live in Kenmore, Washington (near Seattle).
My birthday is August 17; I was born before you were.
2. My books are listed on my website, www.kirbylarson.com.
3. I try to write my stories so readers can take away their own meanings from them.
What do you think the theme is? Write that down and use examples from the book to
support your argument. (Teachers really like this kind of thing.)
4. How do you think the setting influenced the story? Do you think this story would be
the same if it happened in New York City? If it happened in 1965? Write that down and
use examples from the book to support your argument. (Again, teachers go nuts over
this kind of stuff.)
5. I get ideas delivered to me weekly by FedEx. They leave a box on my front porch.
Seriously, I get ideas from everyplace—newspapers, eavesdropping, my imagination.
I also get ideas from emails and letters from readers.
6. The big stuff: I was born and grew up. Along the way, I acquired two college degrees,
two kids, and one husband.
7. See above. Having two kids helps me stay young.
Nope!

Good luck, Ginny! And sleep tight.
Your friend,
Kirby Larson

Dream Book

Ginny's Big Move-to-California List

1. Buy a cute bathing suit
2. Learn to surf
3. Get earphones for cross-country car ride
4. Email Becky Soo every day
5. Get a summer job. Babysit?
6. Teach Grampa Joe how to text
7. Convince Mom to let Brian visit over the summer
8. Keep Henry out of trouble
9. Don't take French next year! (Spanish? Vampirish?)
10. Ignore horoscopes!

PISCES
Change is in the air, Pisces!

FUN IN THE SUN
Carefree California Style is where it's At

VV STUDIOS
Hollywood

HOLLYWOOD

Hi, Becky Soo!
We made it! The car only broke down once, and I got to ride with Grampa Joe and Henry which was great so I didn't have to listen to Ballou cry. We still don't have internet access at the house, so I'm writing you the old-fashioned way, ha-ha. The house we're renting is six blocks from the ocean which is gr8t, but I have to share a bathroom with the boys again which isn't gr8t. Guess what? There's this art studio right down the block and Mom says I can take classes.
Ginny

SURF'S UP!

P.S. Bob says if you visit he'll take us to the new Vampire Vixens theme park in L.A. There's a studio tour too!
AWESOME!!!!!!!!!!

_____

_____

_____

For Montana Posse, future illustrator —J.L.H.
For Aurel Peterson and Dr. Sadismo —E.C.

Text copyright © 2012 by Jennifer L. Holm
Cover art copyright © 2015 by Shutterstock: girl © Piotr Marcinski; desk © STILLFX; pattern © Inga Linder
Interior illustrations copyright © 2012 by Elicia Castaldi

Grateful acknowledgment is made to the following for permission to reprint previously published material:

Candlewick Press, for permission to reprint the book cover from ETERNAL, by Cynthia Leitich Smith, copyright © 2009 by Cynthia Leitich Smith. All rights reserved. Reprinted by permission of Candlewick Press.

Random House LLC, for permission to reprint the book cover from JANE JONES: WORST. VAMPIRE. EVER., by Caissie St. Onge, copyright © 2011 by Caissie St. Onge. All rights reserved. Reprinted by permission of Ember, an imprint of Random House Children's Books, a division of Random House LLC, a Penguin Random House Company.

Henry Holt and Company, LLC, for permission to reprint the book cover from MAKE LEMONADE, by Virginia Euwer Wolff, copyright © 1993 by Henry Holt and Company, LLC. All rights reserved. Reprinted by permission of Henry Holt and Company, LLC.

Visit us on the Web! randomhousekids.com

Educators and librarians, for a variety of teaching tools, visit us at RHTeachersLibrarians.com

The Library of Congress has cataloged the hardcover edition of this work as follows:
Holm, Jennifer L.
Eighth grade is making me sick : Ginny Davis's year in stuff / by Jennifer L. Holm; illustrations by Elicia Castaldi.
   p. cm.
Summary: Eighth grade turns out to be an eventful year for Ginny and her family, as notes, lists, report cards, doctor bills, and other "stuff" reveal that the family moves to a big new house, Brian starts to be more than just a friend, Ginny's mother has a baby, and her stepfather loses his job.
ISBN 978-0-375-86851-1 (trade) — ISBN 978-0-375-96851-8 (lib. bdg.) — ISBN 978-0-375-89920-1 (ebook)
[1. Middle schools—Fiction. 2. Schools—Fiction. 3. Family life—Fiction.]
I. Castaldi, Elicia, ill. II. Title.
PZ7.7.H65Ei 2012 [Fic]—dc22 2011000083

ISBN 978-0-375-87219-8 (pbk.)

MANUFACTURED IN CHINA   10 9 8 7 6 5 4 3 2 1   First Yearling Edition 2015

Random House Children's Books supports the First Amendment and celebrates the right to read.

JENNIFER L. HOLM is the author of three Newbery Honor Books, *Our Only May Amelia*, *Penny from Heaven*, and *Turtle in Paradise*. She is also the author of another book featuring Ginny Davis, *Middle School Is Worse than Meatloaf*, as well as the *New York Times* bestselling novel *The Fourteenth Goldfish* and the Babymouse (an Eisner Award winner) and Squish series, which she collaborates on with her brother Matthew Holm. Jenni lives in California with her husband and two children. She survived eighth grade. Barely.

You can find out more about her by visiting jenniferholm.com or look for her on Twitter at @jenniholm.

ELICIA CASTALDI was born in Providence, Rhode Island, and graduated from the Rhode Island School of Design. She is also the illustrator of Jennifer L. Holm's *Middle School Is Worse than Meatloaf* and *Miss Polly Has a Dolly* by Pamela Duncan Edwards. Elicia divides her time between New York City and Los Angeles. She didn't miss a single day of eighth grade (despite the itchy wool uniform).